I Smell a Rat

Adapted by Mary Olin and Krista Sheffler
Illustrated by Len Smith
Designed by Tony Fejeran and Deborah Boone of Disney Publishing's Global Design Group
Inspired by the art and character designs created by Pixar

Random House 🏠 New York

Copyright © 2007 Disney Enterprises, Inc./Pixar. All rights reserved.
Published in the United States by Random House Children's Books, a division of Random House, Inc., 1745 Broadway,
New York, NY 10019, and in Canada by Random House of Canada Limited, Toronto, in conjunction with Disney Enterprises, Inc.
RANDOM HOUSE and colophon are registered trademarks of Random House, Inc.

ISBN: 978-0-7364-2467-7

www.randomhouse.com/kids/disney

Printed in the United States of America

10 9 8 7 6 5 4 3 2 1

Remy, the rat chef, is out seeking food.
It's such a nice day, and he's in a swell mood.
With Linguini, his friend, Remy sniffs up and down,
Searching the shops for the best treats in town.

Help the rat chef scratch and sniff
the market flowers!

The cheese in this shop looks simply delightful!
Those great big round wheels?
P-U! They smell frightful.

Scratch and sniff the cheese!

That's Emile, Remy's brother. He's found something yummy. It's chewy and sweet, but it looks kind of . . . gummy.

Scratch and sniff the bubble gum!

Now Remy has found a great reason to smile—
Some ripe yellow lemons stacked up in a pile.

Scratch and sniff
the lemons!

Emile's back again! And he's eating a pickle!
If you want to smell him, just give him a tickle.

Tickle Emile and smell his belly!

Brother, it's time for a bath! *Swish, swish, swish.*
Emile gets a washing, just like a dish.
Now that he's clean, Emile's smelling great.
It's time to start cooking. Quick! Grab a plate!

Scratch Emile to sniff his clean scent!

Remy has spied some extra-nice spices.
Next some tomatoes he slices and dices.

Scratch and sniff the spices!

Hurry! Work fast! Dinnertime's near.
Remy chops onions. Emile sheds a tear.

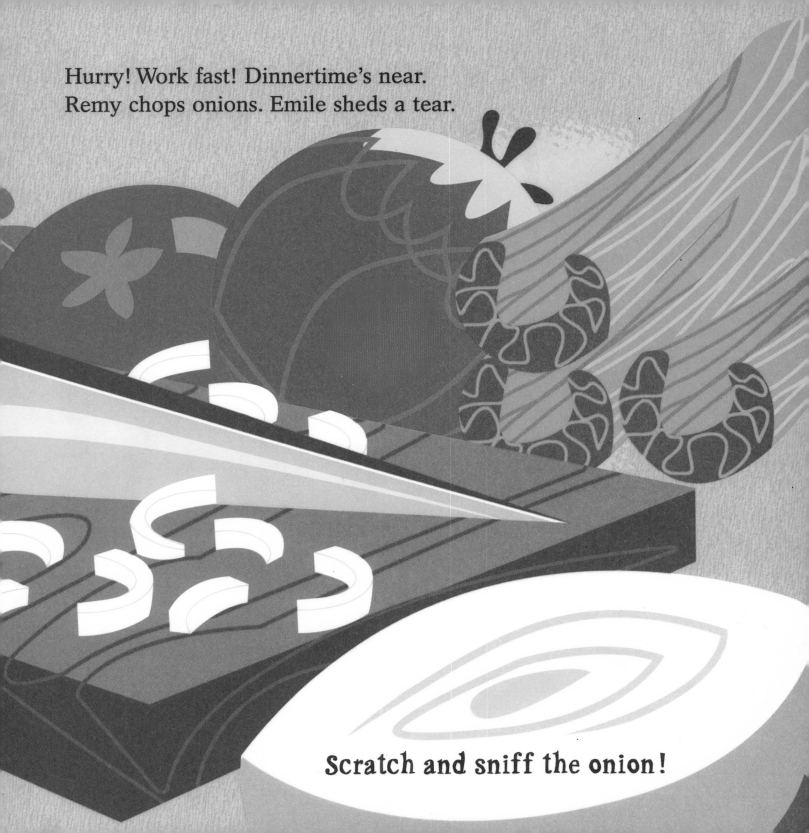

Scratch and sniff the onion!

Ah, lemon, tomatoes, and even some parsley!
Next Remy adds onions and spices quite sparsely.

Scratch and sniff the ratatouille!